Turtle Time

A Bedtime Story

SANDOL STODDARD

Illustrated by Lynn Munsinger

Houghton Mifflin Company

Boston

To Laysan, Max, Allison, and Nick

—S.S.

Walter Lorraine (wr) Books

For information about this and other Houghton Mifflin trade and reference books and multimedia products, visit The Bookstore at Houghton Mifflin on the World Wide Web at http://www.hmco.com/trade/.

Library of Congress Cataloging-in-Publication Data
Sandol Stoddard
   Turtle time / by Sandol Stoddard ; illustrated by Lynn Munsinger
      p.   cm.
   Summary: Climbing into bed, a young child is reminded of the habits of her pet turtle.
   RNF ISBN 0-395-56754-8   PAP ISBN 0-395-85157-2
   [1. Turtles — Fiction. 2. Pet — Fiction. 3. Bedtime — Fiction.
   4. Stories in rhyme.]   I. Munsinger, Lynn, ill. II. Title.
   PZ8.3.S8683Tu   1995   93-39192
   [E] — dc20   CIP
                             AC

Printed in the United States of America
WOZ   10   9   8   7   6   5   4   3

Into my bed for turtle time,
Turtle time.

So now my story's at an end
And one small turtle is my friend.
I don't know what the reason is,
But Fred is mine, and I am his.
And when I hold him in my hand
We close our eyes and understand
Our little song, our little rhyme,
And when I need a nap I climb

And turtle eyes are very wise,
Turtle thoughts are old and deep,
Turtles like to sleep and sleep.
Turtles' dreams are theirs to keep.

And what to eat and how to play
And what to do on a rainy day.

A turtle always knows inside
When to come out, when to hide,
And he knows all he needs to know
Of when to stop and when to go

But pick him up and you will find
That you're too late, you're way behind ...
Turtle time!

And so I learned, and now I see
That Fred is different from me.
A turtle takes a breath of air
To taste what's happening out there,

Turtle space is very small.
It has no furniture at all.
No bed, no chair, no lamp, no shelf.
A turtle lives inside himself.

I may be small, but I am free!
Turtle time is very slow.
It waits until it wants to go.
It has no clocks or rules or maps.
It stops a lot for turtle naps.

But all that day he would not play
I thought that he had gone away
Until at last I heard him say:
Turtle time, turtle time.

And here is what Fred told to me:

I brought my turtle home, and said
Time to come out now—come on, Fred!

And then I picked him up, and heard
A little song without a word:
                    Turtle time, turtle time.
And Fred was round and brown and still.
His back was like a little hill
And he could lie down under it
Because his arms and legs all fit.
His head went in its tiny door.
I couldn't see him anymore.

And for the wintertime, a sled.
I'll keep you underneath my bed
From now on. That is what I said
To Fred.

To drive in—*but,* not very far.

And you will need a little car

And get you turtle toys, a hat,
And shoes, and blankets, and all that.

A raincoat for you to stay dry in

If we both go out to play
Sometime on a rainy day

A tiny bed for you to lie in,

And presents, and a birthday cake,
For being born. And I will make

And find out what you like to eat

And bring you ice cream for a treat

And you're so fresh and neat and new,
I'll make a little house for you

And we were happy. So I said,
I think that I will name you Fred,
And I will bring you home with me
So you can keep me company.

Then out came Turtle, carefully.
I looked at him, he looked at me.

It looked just like a Ping-Pong ball,
Except it wasn't one at all.

One day I saw a turtle egg
Down in the grass with one small leg
Just poking through, and then I found
The shell was cracking all around.

Turtle time, turtle time,
A little song, a little rhyme.
   It always comes into my head
   Whenever I get in my bed
      And cover up and close my eyes.
      Here are the hows and wheres and whys: